Frankly, I NEVER WANTED TO KISS ANYBODY!

The story of THE FROG PRINCE

as told by THE FROG

written by **Nancy Loewen**

illustrated by **Denis Alonso**

Raintree is an imprint of Capstone Global Library Limited, a company incorporated
in England and Wales having its registered office at 7 Pilgrim Street, London, EC4V
6LB – Registered company number: 6695582

www.raintreepublishers.co.uk
myorders@raintreepublishers.co.uk

Text © Capstone Global Library Limited 2014
First published by Picture Window Books in 2014
First published in the United Kingdom in paperback in 2014

Edited by Jill Kalz, Catherine Veitch and Clare Lewis
Designed by Lori Bye
Art Direction by Nathan Gassman
Original illustrations © Picture Window Books 2014
Production by Victoria Fitzgerald
Originated by Capstone Global Library 2014
Printed and bound in China

ISBN 978 1 406 27983 2
18 17 16 15 14
10 9 8 7 6 5 4 3 2 1

British Library Cataloguing in Publication Data
A full catalogue record for this book is available from the British Library.

"You have to kiss a lot of frogs to find your prince."

I bet you've heard that one before. And I bet you're thinking...

EEEWWWWW!

Kissing a frog would be gross!

Well, I just happen to be the frog who inspired that saying. My name is Prince Puckett. And let me tell you, that kiss was no picnic for me either! Here's the REAL story.

I was playing baseball the day
Ben's mum turned me into a frog.
One moment I was about to catch
the ball, which would give my team
the championship...

...and the next moment I was flopping around on the ground with more legs than I knew what to do with.

"Sorry, kid," Ben's mum called as she was led out of the park. "To break the spell, just get a princess to kiss you. But she can't know you're a prince!"

Well, whether I was a prince or a frog, I wasn't about to kiss any girl. And I soon found that being a frog had its perks.

I could see almost all the way around my head.

I could swim and dive like nobody's business.

And wow, could I jump!

I jumped and jumped all the way to a new home, near a well under an old lime tree.

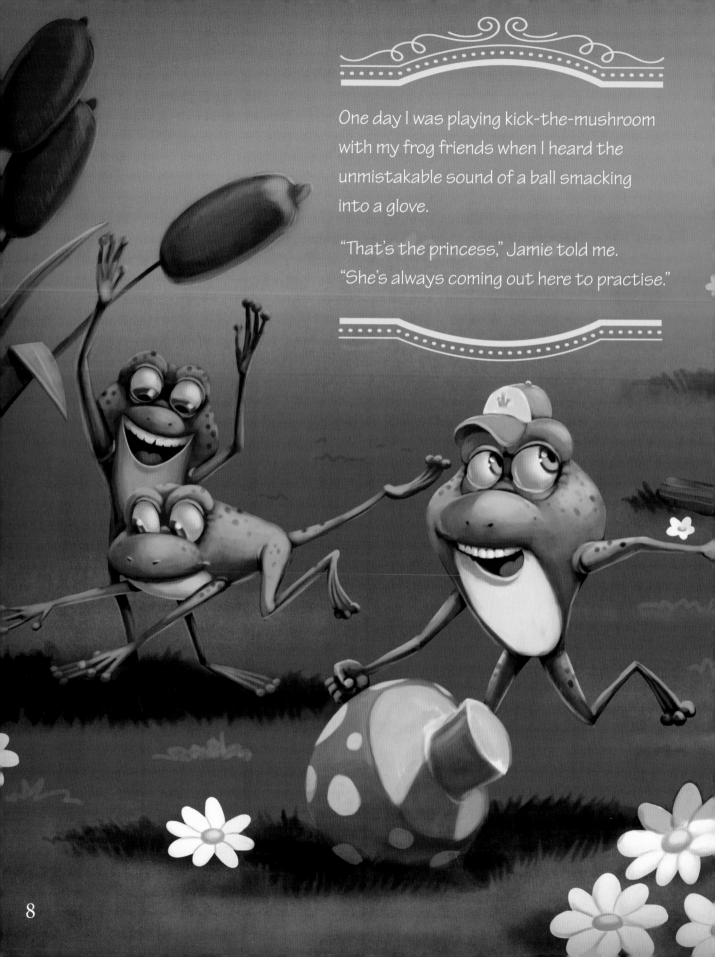

One day I was playing kick-the-mushroom with my frog friends when I heard the unmistakable sound of a ball smacking into a glove.

"That's the princess," Jamie told me. "She's always coming out here to practise."

I listened to the **smack... smack... smack.**
And I wished that I could be just a regular
baseball-playing prince again.

Then it happened.

Smack... smack... PLUNK!

The ball landed in the well.

"That was my lucky ball!" the princess cried.

My friends gathered around me. "If you offer to get the ball, she'll pay you back somehow," Alfie said. "Then you can ask for that kiss."

"Go on," Alex prodded. "Think of your teammates back home."

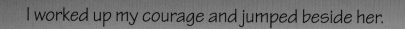

I worked up my courage and jumped beside her.

"Would you like me to get your ball?" I asked.

"You?" she asked. "Well, I guess it wouldn't hurt to try."

I hopped into the well and kicked the ball out.

"How can I ever repay you?" the princess asked.
"Just ask and it's yours!"

"You can … I mean … I'd like a …," I stammered.
Finally I blurted out,

"A kiss! I want you to kiss me!"

"Eeeew!" the princess said.

We stared at each other.

She leaned towards me.

I leaned towards her.

"I can't do it!" she said.
And she took her ball and ran away.

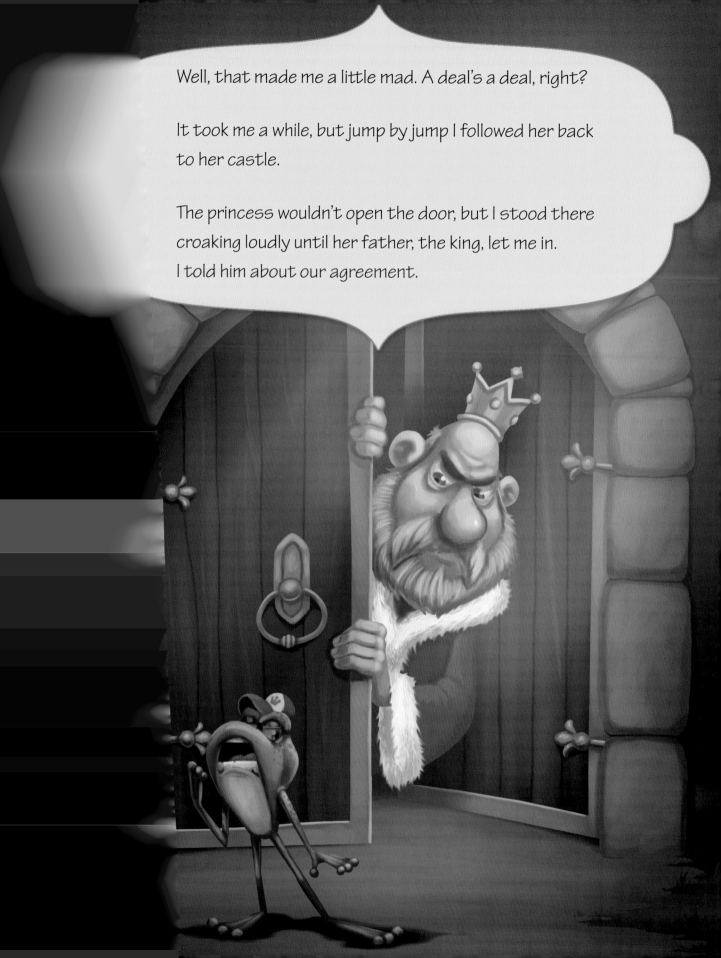

Well, that made me a little mad. A deal's a deal, right?

It took me a while, but jump by jump I followed her back to her castle.

The princess wouldn't open the door, but I stood there croaking loudly until her father, the king, let me in. I told him about our agreement.

"My daughter must keep her word,"
the king assured me in a booming voice.

Then he plopped me down on the dinner table, right next to the princess.

The princess looked the other way. "I'll kiss you after we've eaten," she said. "I promise."

But as soon as she'd swallowed her last bite of apple pie,
she dashed upstairs.

I hopped right after her.

"I'll kiss you just before I go to sleep," she said.
But she pulled the covers over her head and
quickly began to pretend to snore.

I spotted her lucky ball in the corner. "Well, I guess I'll be going now," I said. "Since you won't kiss me, I'll just be taking this."

The princess flung off the covers. "No! Wait! I'll do it!"

She picked me up and held me to her face.

She closed her eyes.

I closed my eyes.

Then... her lips touched mine. **"UGH!"** we both shrieked.

I felt myself being hurled into the air. And suddenly
I was stumbling around with two legs and two arms
that I didn't know what to do with.

"You're a prince!" she said.

"What a throw!" I said.

Did we fall in love, get married, and live happily ever after?

NO WAY. But my team got a great new player!

Think about it

Read a classic version of The Frog Prince. Now look at the frog's version of the story. List some things that happened in the classic version that did not happen in the frog's version. Then list some things that happened in the frog's version that did not happen in the classic. How are the two stories different?

Most versions of The Frog Prince tend to be told from an invisible narrator's point of view. This version is from the frog's point of view. Which point of view do you think is more honest? Why?

If you could be one of the main characters in this version of The Frog Prince, who would you be, and why? One of the frog's friends? The king? The princess? Prince Puckett?

How would other fairy tales change if they were told from another point of view? For example, how would Jack and the Beanstalk change if the giant was the narrator? What if the wolf in Little Red Riding Hood told that story? Write your own version of a classic fairy tale from a new point of view.

Glossary

character person, animal or creature in a story
narrator person who tells a story
point of view way of looking at something
version account of something from a certain point of view

Books in this series

978 1 406 27983 2

978 1 406 27984 9

978 1 406 27985 6

978 1 406 27986 3